The Seed of *Lost Souls*

The Seed of *Lost Souls*

Poppy Z. Brite

Subterranean Press ❁ 1999

ISBN
1-892284-25-1

Subterranean Press
PO Box 190106
Burton, MI 48519

e-mail:
wks@tir.com

Website:
www.horrornet.com/subpress.htm

INTRODUCTION

Late in the autumn of the year 1987, I was a freshman at the University of North Carolina in Chapel Hill, but just barely. I had an eight A.M. linguistics class that I hadn't been on time to once since the semester began. Doing things in the morning has always felt wrong to me. One day I came home from school and put two notebooks side by side on my desk: a looseleaf binder that held my incomprehensible linguistics assignment and a ratty blue spiral-bound job shoplifted from the Student Store, its cover torn off at some point and stuck back on with black electrical tape, that contained the biggest, strangest, most complicated story I'd ever tried to write. And it wasn't finished yet.

Looking at those two notebooks that day, I decided to drop out of college, get a job, and write. I'd been publishing short stories in the small press for two years; this, I sensed, was going to be something more. Leaving school took a huge weight off my heart. The story grew into a novella, and the novella grew into a novel that was published in 1992.

That novel, *Lost Souls*, remains in print seven years after its publication—unusual for a first novel, particularly in the horror genre. It has been published in several languages. It has spawned music, artwork, roleplaying games, devotion, contempt, and a church-sponsored book-burning (though not, contrary to rumor, a movie with Winona Ryder). Here is where it began. Before the prologue (first published in *The Horror Show* as "A Taste of Blood and Altars"), before Steve and Ghost went out robbing Coke machines, before anything else there was this messy, sprawling story, only 7500 words long but encompassing so much territory that I have always called it a novella.

I didn't know anything when I began this story. It was the least *planned* thing I'd ever written, and I've never been much for planning. I had written one story about Steve and Ghost ("Angels"), but I knew little about their history or the North Carolina town where they lived. I had written an unfinished story about Molochai, Twig, and Zillah, but I thought they were a Bowie-esque rock band, not a bunch of vampires. I certainly didn't know that Nothing was Zillah's long-lost son. (I didn't know that when I finished the novella, either; I didn't find out about it until I wrote the prologue in a single rum-drenched night a few months later.)

Many elements from this story were discarded in the first draft *Lost Souls*, most obviously the weird, not-very-well-explained connection between vampires and (of all things) pumpkins. Though it is the supernatural element upon which the novella's plot hinges, it feels forced and doesn't really make sense. It was simply a device, one that seemed creepy to me then but strikes me as silly now, one that allowed me to move these characters around and see how they reacted to one another. The only remnant of it in *Lost Souls* is the scene where Nothing comes to see Steve and Ghost in the graveyard and accidentally flings his lighted jack o'lantern at them. And, of course, Christian selling roses and gourds on the roadside.

Of all the characters who originated in the novella,

Christian is the most changed in the novel. In the first, he is a vaguely sinister cipher; in the latter, a sort of "classic" vampire whose biological difference from the "new" vampires leads to his downfall. The novella suggests that he is some sort of leader; in the novel he is gentler, smarter, and more sentimental than the young vampires, but he is clearly in thrall to them.

Another important differences is Steve and Ghost's attitude toward the vampires. In the novella, Steve simply refuses to believe in them, while Ghost sees them as just another part of the magical world he has always known. While true to their characters, this doesn't allow for much conflict, and so everyone just sort of drifts through the story. In the novel, the two groups are obviously at odds well before Zillah's fateful encounter with Steve's ex-girlfriend Ann. Yet Ghost still feels an empathy with Nothing, though he may wish he didn't, and it's worth noting that even by the end of the novel he still doesn't consider the vampires completely "other." The last line of the novella ("'Angels,' Ghost said.') is echoed in what he says about the vampires in the book's last chapter: "'So maybe they were just like us. I hate what they did, what they do. But they'd hate our lives too. Maybe they did what they had to do to live, and tried to get a little love and have a little fun before the darkness took them.'"

I also added many elements in the transition from novella to novel, most notably the locale of New Orleans. Though *Lost Souls* has come to be known as a "New Orleans book," there are few traces of the city in the novella. This was largely due to a visit I made there in early 1987, after the novella was finished but before I began the massive revision. I hadn't been in several years. I spent the trip wandering the French Quarter, dreaming and drinking in dark little clubs (only one of which, the Crystal, still exists in vastly different form). I met a boy who introduced me to Chartreuse, the little-known, extremely strong, bright green liqueur that has since become a staple in goth bars. I saw how it could all fit into my story, and I came home and began to write it.

I have not chosen to publish this story now, more than ten years later, for its inherent quality: the point of view is all over the place; the plot ranges from oblique to inexplicable; the writing is that of a twenty-year-old, sometimes breathless with possibility but often just breathless. Rather, I offer it as an example of a seed from which a novel grew. It is my fond hope that this artifact will give courage to someone who is just embarking on a novel. This is all I had. I didn't know if I could write a novel. I just knew I couldn't let go of these characters, and so I dove in. When I came out the other side, I had 500 pages and a book deal. Hang on tight.

Poppy Z. Brite
New Orleans, LA
October 1998

THE SEED OF Lost Souls

November 9. A Monday. A cold night outside, the trees he could see through the reflection of his bedroom window tall charcoal sticks shivering, afraid of the wind or only trying to stand against it. Every tree was alone out there. The animals were alone, each in its hole, in its thin fur, and anything that got hit on the road that night would die alone. Before morning, he thought, its blood would freeze in the cracks of the asphalt.

On his scarred and wax-scabbed desk before him lay a postcard. He could not see what the picture was; the design was so intricate, the colors rich enough to blur his eyes. Deep pink the color of mouths, sea green and storm gray, gold embossed in thin bright leaves. It was an optical illusion in color. Its color hid its meaning. He liked that. He picked up his fountain pen with the graceful heart-shaped nib and dipped its delicate tip into the bottle of ink—ink the color of black velvet, with a picture of a spider on the label—and wrote a few spidery lines on the message-side of the postcard:

"Today is the thirty-fourth anniversary of Dylan Thomas' death by whiskey. To you, my angel—my eyes and my voice—a whiskey kiss."

He stretched his legs under his desk and with the bare toes of both feet grasped the bottle he had hidden there. The liquor inside was a darker amber than he was used to, and when he took a swig there was a sharp, smoky taste behind the familiar musky burn that hurt his throat. He swallowed the whiskey, licked his lips to wet them with whiskey and his own clear spit. Then he picked up the postcard and brought it to his mouth and kissed it with his lips and his tongue and all of his passion, kissed it as hungrily as he had ever dreamed of kissing the sweetest, richest mouth. And he picked up the pen again and signed his name.

Nothing

His capital N and the loop of his G swooped like kites' tails. His T was a dagger thrusting down. He took another swig of the whiskey. Apparently the shit from his parents' liquor cabinet was of a far higher quality than the shit his friends poured into empty Pepsi bottles and passed around in a car going too fast on a highway somewhere.

He looked at the postcard, frowned at the signature, the *Nothing* drying dull and black. Why hadn't he signed it in blood? Maybe it wasn't too late. With the pen's tip he jabbed at the soft skin of his wrist until a bead of blood appeared, bright red against his white wrist, with a prick of light from the lamp reflected in it. He signed his name again, *Nothing* in blood, going over the black letters in scarlet. The ink ran into the blood and the whole thing dried rusty brown-black, the color of an old scab. The results did not altogether dis-

appoint Nothing. He felt the thin tickling trickle of blood running down the inside of his forearm, staining the invisible hairs, covering parts of his old scars, leaving parts of their razor-tracery exposed. He licked some of the blood off his arm. It smudged his lips sticky and he smiled at himself in the window reflection. The night-Nothing in the glass smiled back, but coldly, coldly.

Nothing lay on his mattress, which lay flat on the floor (he'd had to fight for that, but the skeleton of his old bedframe and the headboard with the ugly painted cartoon characters stood against the wall in the basement, gathering dust and webs). He watched the planets he'd painted on his ceiling glowing behind the fishnet he had hung up. He felt his room gather itself and stand darkly around him, not frightening but surely full of power. He was never even certain what was in here. Cigarettes, he thought. Flowers from the graveyard. Books, most of them stolen from thrift-shop shelves where he left his finger marks in the dust. Horror stories, thin books of poems, a copy of *Look Homeward, Angel*, on its cover the stone, the leaf, the unfound door. His old stuffed animals. A plastic skeleton whose eyes lit up red if you pulled a cord between its legs. All the objects and pencil drawings on the walls and pictures cut out of magazines formed a web of power around him.

He pulled his quilt up around his legs and touched his ribs, one by one. Good. His hipbones, sharp. He jerked his hand away and pulled the quilt all the way up as the door opened and yellow light from the ceiling lamp spilled down.

"Jason? Are you asleep? It's only nine. Too much sleep is bad for you."

It will block my channels, Nothing thought.

His parents stepped into his room and he felt the web collapse, drift down, broken strands brushing his face. Mother, fresh from her crystal class at the Arts Center, looked exalted. Her eyes sparkled and there was too much blush on her cheeks. Father, behind her, only looked glad to be home.

"Did you do your homework?" Mother asked. "I don't want you going to sleep so early if you haven't done your homework." Nothing turned his head and looked at the pile of textbooks near his closet door. One of the covers was turquoise. One was bright orange. The black T-shirt he'd thrown over them nearly blotted them out.

"Jason, I want to talk to you." Mother came all the way into the room and squatted next to the mattress. Her sweater was of soft iridescent yarn, pink and blue. He saw a smudge of ash from his carpet transfer itself, before his very eyes, onto the knee of her cream-colored trousers. He raised his head to check that the quilt was covering him decently, and thought he saw the small ridges of his hipbones poking up under it.

"I thought of you tonight during our meditation," Mother said. "I don't want to prevent you from expressing your true inner self. You can get your ear pierced after all, if you like. Your father or I will go with you to give permission."

Nothing turned his head to hide the two holes in his earlobe, made with a thumbtack one day at school.

"Wait a minute. Hey. Just what the hell is this?" Father crossed the room in two strides and pulled the whiskey bottle out from under the desk. The last gossamer strands of the web whispered past Nothing's face and dissolved in the light. He smelled the ghost of incense, stayed silent. "Young man, I would like an ex—"

"Just a minute, Roger." Mother radiated benevolence and spiritual wholeness. "Jason is not a bad child. If he's drinking, we should be spending more quality time—"

"Quality time my ass." Nothing decided he liked Father better than Mother these days. "Jason is not a child at all, Marion. He is fifteen and runs with a gang of punks who give him a liquor habit and God knows what else. He dyes his hair. He smokes cigarettes—*Lucky Strikes*," Father said with distaste. "He throws away the clothing we buy him or rips it into rags. Now he's stealing from us. THINGS ARE GOING TO CHANGE AROUND HERE, MARION."

"Roger. We'll talk about it later. Between ourselves. Don't worry, Jason." Mother positively floated out of the room, drawing Father after her. Father slammed the door. A candle fell off a shelf. *If it was lit*, Nothing thought, *I wouldn't get up to put the fire out.* He closed his eyes for a minute and watched the red spangles swirl away behind his lids. Then he got up to turn off the ceiling light, stretching his lithe naked body, shaking his hair and his hands to cleanse himself of Mother's touch.

Father had taken away the good whiskey, but Nothing had his own bottle of brain-rot hidden in the closet. He lay in the dark and drank it, blinking up at the planets. After a while they began to swim. *I've got to get out of this place,* he thought just before dawn, and the ghosts of all the decades of middle-class American children afraid of complacency and stagnation and comfortable death drifted in front of his face, whispering their agreement.

The next day he headed South.

❧

Scratch. Pop, a white-orange flare exploding in the dark.

Steve lit the pipe and sparks showered down, flared like tiny nighttime suns and died among the damp pine needles. When Steve sucked on the pipe, the orange glow turned his dark eyes into deep pools, threw his sharp nose and pointed chin into spooky shadowed relief.

Ghost took the pipe from him. The glow was golden on Ghost's face. It turned his hanging pale hair fiery, suffused his pale blue eyes. He held his breath for a long time and sighed and leaned back against his favorite gravestone. Miles Hummingbird, a private in the Confederate army, killed somewhere in the Virginia woods on a rainy day near the end of the war, trundled home to North Carolina and buried in the springtime mud. Miles' gravestone was rough and gray and moldering, and Miles' bones fell softly away to dust below, and in the drifts of Miles' body lay a shell with creamy pink insides, a shell he had carried home from his family's one trip to the shore when he was twelve, a shell his sister had lain in his hands, over his torn chest, a shell with dry tears inside a hundred and twenty years old. Ghost laid his cheek against the chill granite and thought, *is it cold in the shell tonight, Miles?*, and Miles' rusty Carolina voice, so very far away, said, *It's warm, Ghost. It's warm and yellow as the sand, and the ocean is the color of the sky.*

"What the hell are you thinking about?" Steve asked amiably.

"Long time ago."

"Shit. You ought to be out trick-or-treating, that's where you ought to be. And I ought to be over at RJ's Halloween party with five beers already down and another one ready to go. And here we are in the graveyard gettin' stoned. Shit." Steve lay back in the pine needles with his hands behind his head and regarded the glittering stars above. He looked utterly contented.

"You don't want to go to that damn party. Ann will be there."

Steve didn't reply. The sweet orange smell of singeing pumpkin flesh drifted in from the houses behind the graveyard. Ghost wondered if the one-eyed pumpkin he'd carved was still lit on their porch. "The lost souls get to come out tonight," he said.

"You mean Ann?" Steve lit the pipe again.

"Uh uh." Ghost sucked spicy smoke, felt his lungs tighten and his brain swirl. "All the dark things. All the sad things and the minds left over from the bodies, the minds who don't know they're dead, the ones with no place to go." He felt his pupils grow larger against the dark.

"Now you're tryin' to give me the creeps. All those old ghost stories. Remember 'The Hook?' How the couple hauled ass out of the lovers' lane, and when they got home, the girl found a bloody hook hanging from her door handle? A fine old American legend. Shit, I want a beer. Let's go over to RJ's.

"Shhh." Ghost's head came up; his hair fell over his eyes and he brushed it away. Impatiently, for once. Most of the time he *liked* his hair in his eyes, liked seeing the world through a tangled golden curtain. So Steve, who had known Ghost to try to spook people from time to time but certainly never *him*, sat up and looked into the woods. Something flickered through the pines and kudzu, some bright-orange smudge on the night. A jack o' lantern on somebody's back porch, he guessed. The wind blew, and he shivered.

"There's something out there," said Ghost.

Steve opened his mouth and shut it again. He was going to say something about the weed being good, but he knew Ghost too well for that. Better than he wanted to, sometimes. "OK," he managed in a whisper. "What do we do?"

"Get up quiet. Stay behind me."

Steve grabbed Ghost's arm. He felt Ghost's electricity flowing under his fingers, white and crackling and pure. "Like hell I will. I'm not letting you—"

"Stay behind me," Ghost said again, and looked straight into the woods with his pale eyes, and then branches broke and dead leaves rattled down and something huge and round and fiery was hurtling through the air, and Steve went to

Dame Darcy
1998

the ground fast, pulling Ghost with him. Ghost fell as limply as a rag doll. The fiery orb exploded against Miles' gravestone and ripe pulp spattered them.

"A pumpkin," Steve said. "Fuckin' kids." He pulled up a plant and wiped his face with the leaves.

Ghost licked his lips. "It wasn't kids."

"Huh? Who the fuck was it, then, the Hook?"

"Forget it." All the chunks of pumpkin and pulp looked black in the dark. Steve's lips hadn't been spattered; Steve hadn't tasted the flavor of pennies and life on his tongue, the blood that must have somehow come from inside the pumpkin. Ghost picked a bit of pulp from his eyelash and was silent.

Steve looked at the leaves he was wiping his face with, held them up to the moonlight. "Poison oak. It figures. Shit."

"You won't get it," Ghost told him.

"How—" Steve slapped his knees. "OK. I won't get it. Do we have to wait for somebody to sling a rotting corpse at us, or can we go to RJ's now?"

At the party the lights were bright and RJ wore his round John Lennon glasses over a smudged Dracula face. Steve shoved a tape into the stereo and Tom Waits rasped in his voice of nails and maple syrup, *It's memories that I'm stealing, but you're innocent when you dream, O.* Monica kissed Ghost's cheek and put an icy dripping beer into his hand. He sipped it, tasted the metal of the can and the barley funk, swished it around his mouth and felt blood and pulp mix with the foam. He swallowed that mouthful in a hurry. Then he finished off the can. Tom screamed like a banshee with throat cancer about running through the graveyard with his friends.

We swore we'd be together
Until the day we died . . .

&

Nothing fingered the colored glass bubbles in the divider

between booths of torn maroon vinyl. The Greyhound out of his hometown had taken him down through the Maryland and Virginia suburbs of D.C., down along anonymous highways flanked by chemical processing plants, cigarette mills, housing developments and the dull blue, orange, and green aluminum walls that supposedly held back the noise and smell of the highways.

Now, somewhere deep in Virginia, the roadsides were getting lush and green and the Greyhound had brought him to Good Times Pizza, somewhere south of nowhere, the shrine of the torn vinyl seats and greasy tables and the flashing dangerous jukebox that didn't even have the decency to play mournful country music, that played the ticka-ticka-boom Top Twenty over and over, all day. Nothing held his backpack with his Walkman and his tapes and books close to him. The place reeked of oregano and sour yeast. But the colored glass bubbles were here, beautiful as anything in his room. He wished he could somehow steal just one of them.

He glanced through the window at the bus station across the parking lot, lit a Lucky, tapped it and rubbed ash absently into the thin torn cloth of his jeans. His jeans were soft and comforting, decorated with black swirls of Magic Marker, a chain of safety pins, artistic rips. At the ends of his legs his hightop sneakers chafed each other, tapped together impatiently. There was a hole over one of his little toes.

He took a cassette tape from the pocket of his raincoat and unfolded its paper liner. The liner was a cheap grainy photocopy, one side a picture of an old gravestone surrounded by ivy and pine needles and rough rocks, its surface a jigsaw puzzle of shadow and light. On the gravestone, all 500 copies supposedly lettered by the band themselves, the words **LOST SOULS?** were printed in multicolored crayon. Five colors: magenta, lime green, blue, yellow, black. He imagined each musician clutching one crayon, making his or her particular letter and passing the liner on. RJ lettering perhaps the L and the second O, passing it to Monica, Monica swirling in a green O and U and passing it to Terry, Terry passing it to Steve who surely had the black crayon, Steve finishing off his beer and tossing the liner over to Ghost. Of course Ghost would have had the yellow crayon, and with his fingers would have touched this paper, scrawled an S and the crooked question mark that kept the name from being stupid, S and ? in the color of sunshine.

Nothing turned the liner over and looked at the photo of the band. Small bony RJ, happy Terry, Monica in a black lace mantilla and Steve grinning with a certain easy cynicism. And the other one, the pale one who slid his eyes away from the camera, whose knobby wrists were crossed in his lap, his hands holding something that looked like a cow bone. Whose clothes were too big and whose hair fell from under his straw hat, hiding his face, obscuring him.

All that Nothing knew about the five friends came from this tape, this picture and the long trainwhistle music and the spooky, wistful, exalted words of the songs, and they were his sister and his brothers, the spirits inside his head, the ones he used to wish he was squeezed against on weekend nights, when the car went too fast around a curve and the others yelled for another hardcore tape. Those were teenagers. Nothing knew he was either a child or ancient.

Below the band's photograph was an address, a route number somewhere in North Carolina. Nothing tugged at the drop of onyx in his earlobe, fingered the ballpoint pen in the pocket of his raincoat. Then he unzipped the big compartment of his backpack and dug for his notebook and pulled a postcard out from between the scribbled, burnt, softly ragged pages. The same postcard, the one covered with deep pinwheels and streaks of color. The gold leaf caught the light as he laid the card on the table.

GHOST, he wrote, C/O LOST SOULS?, and copied the North Carolina address.

He finished his cigarette, lit another, looked at his watch, glanced over at the bus station again. It was no good. He couldn't get back on the bus even if he wanted to. The money from his mother's dresser drawer had run out; his stomach hurt and he'd considered spending his last dollar on a slice of pizza, but what if it was the last dollar he ever got in the world? He had to save it for something he wanted, a notebook, a cup of expensive coffee, a black slouch hat in a thrift shop somewhere. You had to spend your last dollar on something important.

He was going to have to start hitching. Something he'd never done before; oh, he'd tried to catch rides from one end of town to the other, but the drivers only looked at his jewelry and lank hair out of the corners of their eyes and passed by fast. Anyway, hitching out on the highway with the bright flat sky stretching away overhead and the great trucks like dragons screaming by, that was a different affair. Anyone might stop for him. A torturer or a religious nut. He liked the torturer better.

Nothing went across the parking lot, dropped the postcard into a faded blue mailbox near the bus station, then climbed up a grassy embankment to the highway. Among the mosaic of dirty gravel and shattered glass on the shoulder was a single long bone, possum or cat, as dry and clean as a fossil. He put it in his pocket.

A pickup truck loomed on enormous tires. Something bloody was lashed to the roof; above the back window of the cab a gun rack bristled. Nothing didn't stick his thumb out. Drunken red faces peered out at him, laughing like dogs. The passenger window cranked down and a glistening amber gob missed his sneaker by a few inches, followed by words guttural and obscene. The wind sucked Nothing's hair over his face and the truck was gone. He wanted to be sick.

An hour's worth of cars and trucks went by, sleek and anonymous, the drivers safe behind windows rolled up against the coming night. Colors melted across the sky, and the sun died its nightly, bloody death. Now the sky was a deep blue-violet away from the lights of the little town, gradually becoming pricked with stars that glittered in his eyes. Nothing began to shiver. He had almost decided to go back and try to sleep in the bus station when the van rolled up to him and stopped.

It was dingy and dusty, black gone to gray. Three heads swiveled to look at him, three clumps of hair, three faces defined in blots of dark makeup. Their hands clawed at the window and their mouths opened, laughing, and for a moment Nothing thought they would drive away and leave him looking after them, his foot already on the asphalt, his skin ready for warmth. But then the passenger door opened and one of the figures swayed toward him, spat hair out of its mouth, and said, "Hi. Wanna ride?"

The air inside the van was as hot and wet as a kiss, and the raw smell of whiskey was so strong he could taste it. Their names were Molochai, Twig, and Zillah. Twig was the driver; he steered with one hand and choked Molochai with the other. Molochai pounded him with grubby fists, then offered him the whiskey bottle. Twig sucked at the bottle and they both giggled wildly as the van swayed across the center line.

Nothing sat on a mattress in the back. Zillah, stretched out next to him, was small with a perfect, sexless face and a ponytail tied back in a purple silk scarf. Wisps of hair hung down, framing that astonishing face, those stunning eyes green as limes, as parrots. Zillah wore a huge black sweater that masked any hint of gender. Nothing wondered. Zillah lit a tiny pipe and passed it to Nothing. It tasted dark and spicy, quite unlike pot.

"What is it?"

Zillah gave him an evil, ravishing smile. "Opium." The husky voice was sexless too.

Nothing lit the pipe again. After a few more drags he tried to touch Zillah's face and missed and said, "You are lovely."

"You are yummy," Zillah told him.

"You're bewitching."

"You're *deathly*."

"Thank you, thank you, thank you . . . " Their mouths met and melted together as Zillah traced runes on Nothing's inner thigh. Nothing slipped his hands under the black sweater and pressed himself to Zillah's flat chest. When

Zillah's long hair fell across his lips, Nothing thought of Ghost. Then he closed his eyes and let himself go. There was an explosion of loud laughter and a tussle in the front seat, and then Molochai put in a tape and the rough voice and the jolting road and the caresses like water carried Nothing away.

You're innocent when you dream, O,
You're innocent when you dream.

❦

"You're in luck. We're going to Missing Mile too. We're meeting our friends there."

"Who are your friends?" Nothing asked hopefully. But Molochai only mumbled "Christian" through his mouthful of cream-filled chocolate cupcake and washed down the stickiness with the cheap red wine that Twig was passing around.

Nothing was severely fucked up. He also couldn't keep his hands off Zillah. The cameo face, the creamy androgynous body drove him mad. Zillah had a purple, yellow, and green streak in his hair—he said he'd been in New Orleans for Mardi Gras last spring—and Nothing braided the streak and put it in his mouth and ran his hands under Zillah's sweater and bit the back of Zillah's neck. Molochai and Twig laughed at them and opened another bottle of wine.

They were parked in a field somewhere in southern Virginia, or maybe in North Carolina. But they couldn't be in Carolina yet, because Ghost was there and Nothing would surely have felt his presence as the van crossed the state line. He cleared a spot on the foggy window with his sleeve, saw corn and stars outside. The window was cold against his hand. He put his cheek on the glass and realized how hot his face was, how hot his whole body was. Then he was fumbling at the door handle and Molochai said, "Just puke in this bag here, it's Twig's," but Nothing fell out of the van and rolled over the crackling dead cornstalks and vomited rich and copiously on the frosty earth. He choked, spat, watched as the steam from his vomit washed over his face. Dimly he became aware that Zillah was holding him, that Zillah's white hands were smoothing his hair back from his burning face.

"I *hurt,*" he told Zillah.

"Mmm," Zillah agreed. "I know."

Back in the van, Molochai and Twig didn't rib him; they were snuggled quietly on the mattress, clutching each other like children. Nothing lit a Lucky, but wrinkled his nose and put it out after a few drags.

"Still sick?" said Molochai. "We've got something to make you feel better." He reached under the mattress and found a dirty bottle half full of something dark, ruby, thicker than wine. "This will put you right. If it doesn't kill you."

"What is it?"

"An indescribably peculiar potion," Twig told him. "Something distinctly strange. Something like—" He shut up when Molochai stuck grubby fingers in his mouth.

Nothing took the bottle, uncapped it, lifted it to his mouth and sipped. He took the bottle away, then lifted it again and drank deep. Molochai, Twig, and Zillah watched him, very still, as if they

were holding their breaths. Nothing stopped drinking and licked his lips and smiled at them.

"I don't think drinking blood is so strange," he said. He showed them the scars on his forearms. The others reacted at once, laughing, cheering him, punching him and ruffling his hair.

"He's OK!" said Molochai joyfully, and planted a sticky kiss on Nothing's forehead. He pushed the bottle to Nothing's lips again. They passed it around, drank until the insides of their mouths were stained rotten red.

When the sky began to lighten, the birth of morning found them heaped on the mattress, limbs tangled, hair across faces, hearts to backbones, hands clutching hands. Zillah stirred and muttered as the light touched his eyelids. He pressed his mouth back against Nothing's soft throat and had to suck like a baby before he could sleep.

"For fuck's sake, Ghost, it's going to snow. Sling your bike in the back of the T-bird and I'll drive you into town."

"I don't need a ride. I'm dressed warm." Ghost pulled his drab layers of clothing around him. "I like the wind in my eyes."

"Suit yourself. Keep your hat on your head." Steve pushed the straw hat more firmly down over Ghost's long hair, tugged the colored ribbons that spilled from the brim. "Call me if you get icicles on your balls. I'll come pick you up."

The wind sluiced over Ghost's face, froze the winter-tears in his eyelashes, whistled through the spokes of his bicycle wheels like a lonely song. His hair whipped his face, pale and cold. The streets of Missing Mile were deserted this twilight, the shops in town dark behind dusty glass, the homes on the hills checkered with yellow-lit windows.

He did his errands in town, then took the long way home. The fields were bare and dry, stripped of their harvest. At the corner of the highway, just before he swung onto his own long road, a lone angular figure huddled behind a flower stand. ROSES, said the painted wooden sign. The flowers shivered in the wind. Around the base of the stand were clustered a few stunted pumpkins and gourds. Left over from Halloween, Ghost guessed.

As he slowed his bike to a stop, the figure behind the stand stood and spread its arms wide. It was wearing some kind of long dark robe; the sleeves billowed. The moon was in the sky, suddenly, it seemed. Ghost hadn't noticed it rising.

"Flowers? Or a candle?"

"I don't know. I stopped because I felt sorry for you. You ought to pack it up for tonight. Too cold, and nobody ever drives out here."

"Pity? For pity's sake you can have a rose, friend." The figure stepped closer and tucked a scarlet bud into the lapel of Ghost's secondhand army jacket. At the touch of the long thin fingers he shivered; they had brushed the bare triangle of skin at the base of his throat, and they were terribly cold. He raised his eyes and looked into the face. In this light he could hardly tell, but there seemed to be a cross drawn in makeup or tattooed on the high pale forehead. The eyes glittered deep in their sockets, and Ghost looked quickly down at his own dirty white sneakers. The gourds caught his eye with their autumn colors.

"I'll buy a couple of those," he said, choosing a long yellow one and a green one speckled with deep orange. The man—Ghost thought it was a man, judging from the prominence of veins and tendons in the hands—took the gourds and shoved them into a wrinkled paper bag. Ghost paid and rode away, the moon at his back. Once he stopped and looked over his shoulder, but the stand and the lonely figure, if still there, were hidden in shadow.

When he got home, Steve's car was gone. Ghost turned on all the lights and put the gourds in the middle of the living room floor. He lay on the sofa and looked at them, feeling as if he'd brought a little of the darkness inside with him.

He saw the yellow gourd poised above his face, toppling.

The green gourd split open with a wet ripping sound and its innards ran red across the floor. The wind-driven moonlight rattled the lock on the front door. Although he knew all this was happening, he couldn't open his eyes to see it.

Ghost awoke still looking at the gourds. They sat where he had left them, smooth and intact. His cheek felt hot and creased by the sofa cushions. He lifted his head. The lock was still rattling. Was it the wind? No, someone was knocking, hard and frantically, then twisting the knob.

"Ghost! Open the fuckin' door!" Something that sounded suspiciously like the toe of a cowboy boot kicked at the wood. Ghost opened the door and Steve spilled over the threshold, long arms and legs and tangled black hair and dire curses. Ghost shut the door fast to keep the dark out. Steve fell back on the couch and draped his arm dramatically over his eyes. Ghost went into the kitchen and got two beers from the refrigerator. Steve accepted his gratefully and sucked at it like a man demented by thirst.

Neither spoke until they were on their second round of beers. Then Steve said, "You know that crazy jack o'lantern you carved for the porch?"

Ghost took a big swallow of beer and didn't answer.

"Well, that's why I was out. I threw that thing in the compost heap last week. Today, right after dark, I walked up the driveway to get the mail. When I came back, the damn jack o'lantern was back on the porch, and it was lit. Burning. I could see the eye and the mouth from halfway up the drive, and I could smell the pumpkin roasting. And then I realized I was so spooked that I didn't even want to walk past it into the house. I was all looking behind me and then turning back around because I didn't want to look away from it. But I came in and grabbed my keys and went out looking for you."

"I took the long way home."

"Yeah, I figured. So—pretty stupid, huh? Oh yeah, and there was some mail for you." Steve reached into his coat pocket and pulled out a postcard, bent and dog-eared, its bright colors muted with the grime of small-town post offices.

"Whiskey kiss," Ghost read aloud. "Nothing." He looked up at Steve. "Who knows?"

"Why don't you hold it to your forehead and find out? Go on, tell me to fuck myself."

"Suck my aura," said Ghost, and smiled.

ᘜ

It was several beers later. The lights seemed brighter now. The darkness outside was only night, and sometime toward morning the sky would grow pale again. "Let's play the tape," Steve suggested, and their music jangled through the rooms of the house. Ghost sang along with his own golden-gravel voice. Steve picked up his guitar and banged at the strings; there was a fiery, chiming melody beneath the noise. Soon the beer and the exuberance and the music made them too drunk to sit and listen. Ghost pulled Steve up and they reeled around the living room, laughing helplessly, falling on each other. Steve tripped over his own feet. The toe of his boot connected with the green gourd and sent it flying against the wall. It split open and left a dark red stain on the plaster. The music ended. The silence was louder.

"Is it supposed it look like that?" Steve asked finally.

"Like what?"

"So . . . red. And what are those lumps? What the hell is that thing, Ghost?"

Ghost walked over and looked at the broken shell of the gourd. Red beads of moisture bled slowly from the exposed edges of the flesh. He touched the stain on the wall, then shook his head.

Their bodies had not yet caught up with the sudden sobriety of their minds. The effect was a rolling and remote dizziness. They walked in very straight lines, and their eyes were big like those of children in the dark. They kept their hands steady as they wiped the stain from the wall, cleaned the mess off the floor, and dumped it all in the garbage pail.

Outside, the one-eyed pumpkin still flickered in the late night. Ghost wouldn't let Steve blow it out. "Maybe it's guarding us," he said. Truth was, he didn't know what might happen if the flame died before morning.

ᏋᏗ

"Wake up! We're there!"

Nothing opened and shut his eyes several times. The watery afternoon light was like a million fireworks pouring through the windows of the van, like a white flame explosion in his head. His mouth was parched; he thought he could feel each individual brain cell shrieking its protest against the light. He looked away from the window and into the face of Molochai, who had crawled into the back to shake him. Molochai's eyes glittered, surrounded by enormous smudges of dark makeup. Nothing smelled something sweet on Molochai's breath, some buried childhood odor. Twinkies.

"Hey kiddo! We're there. Here. In Missing Mile. Route two, box 7-A, right?"

"Right." Nothing held his backpack close to him. The streaky faces of Molochai and Twig hung over him, haggard and grinning, waiting to see what he would do. "If you want to stay here," Twig told him, "we're dropping you off. We have to meet our friends."

"You can come," Molochai offered. "It's not often we meet a drinking man like you."

Where was Zillah? Asleep there on the mattress, his warmth close enough to touch, his head nestled in his arms. Wisps of his dry Mardi Gras hair trailed away over his hands. But route two, box 7-A was the address on the Lost Souls? tape. Ghost might be here, in that house at the end of the long gravel driveway. "I have to get out here," he told them. "Will you be in town long?"

"Maybe. You think you might want to find us? Check with one of those people who sell roses on the sides of the road. They all know us." And then Nothing was standing unsteadily in the gravel driveway and the dusty black van was pulling away. Molochai's ratty clump of hair popped out the window and Molochai threw something glittering that turned end over end and fell at Nothing's feet. The van was gone. Nothing picked up the half-empty flask of whiskey and put it in the pocket of his raincoat.

He turned to face the house and started walking. It was thirty steps away, twenty. Scruffy gray wood, ragged shutters. Someone had painted a hex sign, or something like one, at the threshold of the front door. A red triangle and a blue one interlocked to form a six-pointed star; in the center, a small ankh was traced in silver paint. A green street sign, FINN ROAD, was nailed to one of the porch posts. Half a coconut shell hung on a string by the door. When Nothing knocked with it, timidly and then loudly, no one came.

The window next to the door was wide open, though, and there was an old brown car in the driveway. Somebody must be here. He couldn't just let himself in, couldn't just climb through the window no matter how cold the wind that cut across the porch, no matter how much he wanted to see what was inside Ghost's house. He couldn't go in the window, he *couldn't*. A bit of red pulp from the sill stained the leg of his jeans as he hoisted himself in.

The obscure, lovely acid rock posters and the bookshelf full of Jack Kerouac, Ray Bradbury, Harlan Ellison and the landscape of beer cans that led from the kitchen around the couch and away down the hall captured Nothing's attention for several minutes before he noticed the smell. When it finally entered his sphere of awareness—he was in Ghost's house; there was Steve's banjo in the corner; Ghost had surely sat on that couch, on that dirty yarn coverlet—he could not decide whether it was an unpleasant smell or only a strange one. No, it wasn't strange, it was familiar. A rare smell, though. Another buried odor from childhood, mellower than Molochai's Twinkies and more rotten, more pungent, more *orange* . . .

The organic mold-laced smell of a jack o'lantern left to

rot on a porch or in a compost heap long after Halloween. And under that, the smell of wet pennies.

The hall was very long and palely lit by the open rooms. Nothing turned off the light in the bathroom as he passed, looking at the ivory-yellowed porcelain, the tub standing on gryphons' feet, the lone beer can on the edge of the sink. He was seeing things clearly, slightly removed, very aware of where he was. He was in the house of Ghost. He was only looking at things. But when he came to the open doorway of a bedroom, he stopped and shut his eyes and fell to his knees.

After several seconds he opened his eyes and looked again at the two young men there, one stretched limply on the bed, one half tumbled to the floor, among the empty cans. And then Nothing crawled to the bed and began kissing, no, *licking* the dark blotches off the fair dreaming face. Tears ran from his eyes and fell among the tangles of Ghost's hair.

Steve muttered and raised his head and saw Ghost, his army jacket rumpled and stained, the rose now full-blown in his lapel, the strange boy with lank black hair bent over him, crying and licking his face. Ghost's face was dark and wet with pulp, with blood. Steve's hangover left him. He pulled himself up to his full stringy height and screamed Ghost's name once, twice, grabbed the black-haired boy by the front of his raincoat, and threw him across the room.

Ghost's eyes stayed shut; his breaths were slow and shallow and far between; his eyelashes were scraps of satin on his cheeks. Steve, sobbing, wrenched Ghost's mouth open and began raking out the chunks of bloody pumpkin pulp stuffed inside. "What the fuck," he managed, "what did you—I'll kill—fuckin' hell—"

Nothing's forehead was bleeding where he had hit a guitar stand. A thick red rivulet ran down his face, and he put his tongue out and licked it up. The taste reminded him of the bottle that he had shared with Molochai, Twig, and Zillah. Maybe they'd found their friends who sold roses.

He looked at the rose in Ghost's lapel. Red pulp delicately webbed the petals. "Steve," he said.

Steve, his fingers still in Ghost's mouth, glared up at Nothing.

"I didn't hurt him. I swear to any God you like I didn't. I came in your window because—" Nothing couldn't think of anything adequate to say here, so he took the flask out of his pocket and drank a long swig. Its burn comforted him. "Steve, I think you better take the rose out of his jacket. I think it might be killing him." When Steve didn't move, Nothing came slowly forward and reached for the rose. Steve made as if to strike him, but Nothing, unflinching, took the rose between thumb and forefinger and pulled it out of Ghost's lapel. "This is *my* birthright," he said, and smiled at Steve as he tucked the rose into the top buttonhole of his own coat.

Ghost's eyelids fluttered. He saw himself reflected twice in Steve's scared dark eyes. "I dreamed about vampires," he said.

"Vampires?" Steve looked up at Nothing. "Kid, are you in some kind of trouble?"

"No." Nothing took another swig of his whiskey, offered it to Ghost and Steve. Ghost rinsed his mouth out, spat the first mouthful into a beer can, took another. Steve tipped the bottle up and handed it back fingerprinted with the pulp and spit from Ghost's mouth. Nothing lit a Lucky Strike. "No," he said again. "I'm not in any trouble."

"When there are vampires," Ghost said slowly, "you have to kill them." His pale blue eyes met Nothing's and clouded. "Unless—"

Nothing touched his own throat. "Unless."

"Be careful," said Ghost. He thought of the postcard that had come yesterday. "Be careful, Nothing."

"Don't worry. Halloween is over now." Nothing stepped backward into the hall. "And I promise I won't bite anyone who doesn't want to be bitten." He raised the whiskey bottle, turned, and was gone.

ꕤ

The figure stood up dark and angular behind the flower stand, his back to the rising moon. The moon was nearly new, a sliver, a hole edged with light in the sky. "Flowers?" said the figure. "Or a candle?" Something in the boy's face alerted him, and he stopped.

"Christian?" said Nothing.

"How do you come?"

"In peace." The tip of Nothing's cigarette glowed. "With a drink." He held out the nearly empty bottle, and Christian took it, drained it, shivered slightly and smiled.

"Can you give me something to eat?" Nothing asked. Christian took a knife from inside his robe and cut open one of the small pumpkins. They fed together in silence. When they had finished, Nothing leaned over to Christian and delicately, with his lips and the tip of his tongue, kissed the dark cross on Christian's forehead. He held Christian's cold hand. And sometime later the black van pulled up, and Molochai, Twig, and Zillah leaned out laughing, howling, inviting. And the music played. And inside the van was light and warmth and blood.

Steve and Ghost sat on the front porch and finished off a twelve-pack. Steve talked lovingly about what a piece of shit the T-bird was, how he was going to sell it for scrap metal next week. Ghost watched the night sky. After a while he spoke:

"And I saw a star fall from heaven unto the earth: and to him was given the key of the bottomless pit. And he *liked* it there."

Steve turned, shook his head. "Huh? What the hell, Ghost . . . *vampires*?"

"Angels," Ghost said.

November 1987 - January 1988
Chapel Hill, North Carolina

A Book Review

[NOTE: This book review was commissioned and purchased by the VLS, but they never ran it. I'm publishing it here because it's relevant to the subject and I still like it.]

Vampires, Wine and Roses by John Richard Stephens

New vampire books turn up in my mail every two weeks or so. They make me cranky, because I don't like vampires very much. I am only guilty of producing one actual work about bloodsuckers and their ilk, my novel *Lost Souls,* published in 1992 and mostly written long before that. Even then, I wasn't especially interested in vampires *per se*; I ended up writing about them because they were an essential icon of the Goth subculture I wished to portray, a symbol of death's beauty and heady sexuality. Even then, I found them kind of irritating.

More recently, I edited two anthologies of erotic stories about vampires. I wouldn't have chosen vampires—the publisher came to me with the idea—but I jumped at the chance to publish a bunch of good short work by writers I admired. I deliberately chose writers who weren't known for vampire fiction, many who weren't even known as horror writers. *Love In Vein 1* and *2* made money and gained exposure for several of the writers, but for me, they were the seal of doom: I am now, indisputably, a Vampire-Associated Author. Henceforth until the end of time, people will assume I am still interested in vampires, and they will send me books about them. This one, *Vampires, Wine & Roses* is a reprint anthology edited by John Richard Stephens: some standard stuff, some unusual material. Who knew Shakespeare wrote about vampires?

Well, he didn't, actually. Stephens has hauled out an excerpt from *Romeo and Juliet,* a seventeen-line balcony exchange that ends with the barest hint of a vampire metaphor ("Dry sorrow drinks our blood. Adieu, adieu!").

This credibility-stretching opener is followed by a dismal short story and two tiresome sets of lyrics. Anne Rice is responsible for all of these, though she only wrote the first two: "The Master of Rampling Gate," a sort of mini-vampire-Harlequin Romance first published in *Redbook,* and "The Ballad of the Sad Rat," a country song written from the point of view of a rat on the set of *Interview With A Vampire.* ("I'm a HOLLYWOOD RAT / in a HOLLYWOOD MOVIE! / WHAT WOULDN'T YOU GIVE / TO TAKE MY PLACE?") Rice's megalomania is exceeded only by her penchant for capital letters. The third offering is Sting's "Moon Over Bourbon Street," inspired by Rice's novels. These lyrics are not bad, but by now I am too annoyed with the whole idea of Anne Rice to appreciate them.

It can only get better from here, and does. While several of the short stories Stephens selects have been frequently reprinted, most of them are a pleasure to re-read. Poe's "Ligeia," de Maupassant's "The Horla," H.G. Wells's "The Flowering of the Strange Orchid," Bradbury's "The Homecoming," R.L. Stevenson's "Olalla," Stoker's "Dracula's Guest," and Lovecraft's "The Hound" will all be familiar to fans of weird fiction, but seeing them in this context underscores the diversity of the vampire tale. And therein, I think, lies the eternal appeal of the vampire tale: it always comes back to blood and sex, but it can be told a million different ways.

As always happens when I read a really good vampire story—when I am reminded that there *is* such a thing, however rare it may be—I realize that I don't really dislike vampires. In my introduction to *Love In Vein,* I wrote that "the vampire is everything we love about sex and the night and the dark dream-side of ourselves: adventure on the edge of pain, the thrill to be had from breaking taboos." I still believe that, or at least believe that it can be possible. I don't think the vampire genre can be expanded—it has said everything it can say in any number of ways—but I do think wonderful things can still be done with it.

So I don't dislike vampires; I just dislike 99 percent of what has been written, filmed, drawn, and theorized about them, and that keeps me from reading much contemporary vampire writing. The last interesting vampire novel I read, *The Five of Cups* by Caitlín R. Kiernan, is not on any publisher's upcoming list. Kiernan's first novel, *Cups* was purchased by Transylvania Press, a Vancouver house specializing in vampire literature, but they folded before publishing it. Now Kiernan is so disgusted by the current state of vampire fiction that she has decided not to market *Cups* for the time being. Her second novel, *Silk,* was published by Roc in 1998. There are no vampires in it.

For it is a bad thing to get pegged as a vampire writer. There's this weird obsessiveness about vampires that makes writing about them dangerous if you only want to do it once. Everybody—readers, editors, role-playing-game geeks—will want and expect you to do it again and again and again. There are people out there who will buy *absolutely any book about vampires.* That's what causes books like *Vampires, Wine & Roses.* I'm not inherently opposed to this phenomenon. It's supply and demand, and, hey, it's been kind to me.

Stephens obviously cares about his subject enough to

have dug up some obscure material: in addition to the short stories, there is a selection of vampire poetry. Though this is an inherently cringe-inducing phrase, conjuring up images of badly illustrated, blackly Xeroxed zines dripping with teenage angst, the works herein run the gamut from sublime (Goethe's "The Bride of Corinth") to pathetic (F. Scott Fitzgerald's "The Vampires Won't Vampire for Me," written while he was in college; its inclusion here must be a sore embarrassment to his wraith).

One of Stephens's real finds is an excerpt from the first printed version of T.S. Eliot's *The Wasteland,* first published in 1922. The lines refer to the chilling scene in the novel *Dracula* where Jonathan Harker sees the Count crawling down the castle wall:

A woman drew her long black hair out tight
And fiddled whisper music on those strings
And bats with baby faces in the violet light
Whistled, and beat their wings
And crawled head downward down a blackened wall
And upside down in air were towers
Tolling reminiscent bells, that kept the hours
And voices singing out of empty cisterns and exhausted wells.

Other pleasant surprises include a classic weird tale by Edith Wharton and a scathingly sarcastic essay by Voltaire on the problem of vampires in the Catholic church.

For me, though, the real pick of the litter is Ivan Turgenev's "Phantoms," published in 1864. The narrator is plagued by a melancholy flying succubus named Alice who whisks him all over Europe, professes great love for him, and even resurrects Caesar—ostensibly for his edification, but our angst-ridden hero is stricken with terror when "a pale stern head, in a wreath of laurel, with downcast eyelids, the head of the emperor, began slowly to rise out of the ruin . . . I felt that were that head to raise its eyes, to part its lips, I must perish on the spot! 'Alice,' I moaned, 'I won't, I can't, I don't want Rome, coarse, terrible Rome . . . Away, away from here!'" ("Coward!," she answers appropriately, and spirits him off to Italy.)

"Phantoms" is easily one of the strangest stories I've ever read. I am surprised and delighted to find it in a vampire anthology. The vampire is the easiest horror trope to turn into a cliché, and yet a great many writers try their hand at a vampire tale sooner or later, maybe because the familiar canvas can show off one's individual flourishes so well. To write about a creature that lives off the human life-force requires the ability to plumb one's own darkness.

To enjoy reading about them also requires an attraction to darkness (and a prurient one at that, as it is very difficult for vampires *not* to be sexual). Conrad Aiken touches upon this need in an excerpt from his poem "The Divine Pilgrim:"

Vampires, they say, blow an unearthly beauty,
Their bodies are all suffused with a soft witch-fire,
Their flesh like opal . . . their hair like the float of night.
Why do we muse upon them, what secret's in them?
Is it because, at last, we love the darkness,
Love all things in it, tired of too much light?

Anyone who has ever loved vampires—even if, like me, they are reluctant to own up to that dark fascination now—will understand these lines, and will probably be reminded of a favorite vampire story or two.

My own flashbacks upon reading Aiken's passage were George R.R. Martin's *Fevre Dream* (1982)—possibly the finest vampire novel ever written—and *The Rocky Horror Picture Show* (laugh if you will, but Dr. Frank N. Furter, with his weary, defiant glamour, was my favorite movie vamp ever).

John Richard Stephens has demonstrated that the history of vampire writing is as obsessive, patchy, diverse, and occasionally brilliant as its current state. More important, he has compiled a thought-provoking and mostly entertaining volume. Despite the weak beginning and some thin material, *Vampires, Wine & Roses* makes a good bedside vampire reader even if you don't like vampires—or don't think you do.

January 1997
New Orleans, LA

An Interview

Interviewed for *Blue Blood,* 1993
by Jon Von Faust

What were you like as a child? Were you a loner or more of a recluse? Where did you attend high school? Did you attend college, if so what did you major in?

I learned to read at age 3 and haven't stopped since. I've also been writing and drawing since I can remember. I was always fascinated by guts, blood, and bodily functions, as I think most kids are, but I just never gave it up. I spent a lot of time alone by my own choice, but I usually had a couple of other weird kids around to subvert. It wasn't until junior high that they all began to hate me, because that is the age when everyone must conform, and I was never any good at that. I attended the loathsome Jordan High School in Durham, North Carolina for three years, during which time I published *The Glass Goblin,* the school's first underground paper. I was branded a Commie and received death threats in my locker and such, but I also made some people *think* about things they probably never would have otherwise, and I became addicted to that feeling.

I dropped out midway through my senior year and

worked for two years, during which time I published my first short stories. Then I went back and finished high school in Chapel Hill, which was slightly better, but by that time I had gone all deathly and suicidal. I would come to school with blood smeared around my eyes and all. I'm convinced I only survived that year because of Dylan Thomas, William S. Burroughs, T.S. Eliot, Samuel Beckett (*Waiting for Godot*), the Cure, Bauhaus, and Gene Loves Jezebel (centuries ago when they were good). And my few friends and my mom, of course.

I attended college at UNC-Chapel Hill for all of two months before dropping out to write *Lost Souls*. I knew I didn't have time for both, and there was really no contest. Never went back, never wanted to. I advise all creative writers to stay as far away from large universities as possible. They want to teach you *exactly how to write*; they do not take into account that you might already know a thing or two about it; and in the process they will try their best to kill your soul.

When did you first become interested in writing?

In the womb, as far as I can tell. I've been doing it since I could hold a pen and make words. I've been writing seriously—that is, trying to improve my work and get it published—since I was 12, and I sold my first short story at 18 to *The Horror Show* magazine.

Do you yourself believe in vampires? If so, why?

I usually believe in almost anything until it is disproved to me, and even then I sometimes keep believing. Vampires aren't as high on my list of belief as, say, ghosts or the Bermuda Triangle, but I wouldn't be terribly surprised if I met some, either. I'm a Subgenius, praise "Bob," and we're very good at pulling the wool over our own eyes.

However, if you genuinely believe you *are* a vampire, please don't come up to me at a party and tell me about it. I won't believe you, and it's a lousy pickup line.

How did you obtain a contract with Abyss Books? What kind of royalties do you get from *Lost Souls?*

I started writing *Lost Souls* partly because another publisher had expressed interest after reading some of my stories in *The Horror Show.* The first draft was actually written between November '87 and October '88. By the time the publisher decided their horror line wasn't going to happen, my friend Brian Hodge had just sold his third novel to Abyss, and he offered to show my manuscript to his editor. She liked it a lot. By that time I had an agent, Richard Curtis. After Abyss made an offer, Richard conducted an auction for the book, which means several different publishers bid on it and Abyss had the right to top the highest bid by 10%, which they did. Originally they were going to publish *Lost Souls* as part of their successful paperback line. When they decided to make it the first Abyss hardcover, I signed a separate contract for that and my next two books.

Publishers tend to get a little upset if authors talk about the amount of their advances, their royalties, and such in interviews, so I'd better just say I'm well taken care of.

On the jacket cover of your book it says you were an exotic dancer. Do you feel that this line of work exploits women or is it really the pathetic men who patronize this sort of position who are really being exploited?

Yes. Both. And neither. I mean, last time I checked, I didn't see anyone in the stripclub dressing room holding a gun to the dancers' heads, forcing them to keep the job. They make good money. It's a stressful job and it's hard work; strippers aren't just these helpless little dolls up there onstage being exploited. Some of them have a lot of fun with it. Some are putting themselves through school or keeping themselves alive to do their real work, as I was; some make enough money to start stock portfolios and retire by thirty. I don't call that exploitation. And I don't think I'd want to *date* the kind of man who goes to strip clubs, but not everyone I met was a pathetic asshole or idiot, either. Most of them are either out with a bunch of friends doing their male bonding, or else they're just lonely guys who hardly deserve to be picked on by a bunch of humorless so-called feminists (of either gender). Sure they're getting ripped off, but we live in a capitalist society.

What compelled you to write *Lost Souls*?

It just grabbed me by the throat and didn't let go for 469 pages.

Would you classify *Lost Souls* as a horror story or do you feel it is more purely a vampire story? (I realize that this is one and the same to some people; however, most of the people reading this interview find vampires erotic, sexy, and would probably give their mother's soul to be one.)

According to *Lost Souls,* if you're a vampire then your mother is long dead, so I guess they're out of luck. Sure, vampires are erotic and sexy—but any kind of horror can be erotic and sexy! Check out the novel *Frisk* by Dennis Cooper. It's about a gay serial killer who loves to fuck, torture and mutilate these pale, skinny boys that look like the actor Keanu Reeves, and it is *hot.*

I write about a lot besides vampires, but I almost always like to find the erotic side of whatever story I'm telling. Sex can be scary, disturbing, disgusting. Moreover, it can be all of those things and still be *very sexy*! I guess there are people who would draw a dividing line, but I'm not sure I can, at least not with *Lost Souls.* It's the story of those characters, and what happens to them could not have happened any other way. Some of it's quite horrible, some of it is sexy, some is both. I'm not much for drawing lines where there don't need to be any.

When you wrote *Lost Souls* did you have any demographic group in mind or were you writing it for a

general audience?

I wrote it for a demographic group of one: myself. It is extremely gratifying when others enjoy my work, but I don't try to aim it at some preconceived audience. I can't. I write what I have to, what I love. If it reaches people who can also love it and use it, great—but if I was in a cave somewhere in Tibet, I'd still be doing it.

The insight you have about the gothic scene is indicative of someone who has spent a lot of time either observing or participating in the underground or gothic movement. Were you ever a gothic rock fan? Did you go to underground clubs? Which ones?

Well, I've seen the Cure four times! I like gothic rock a lot, actually, and as I told you before, I still wear the old black. But I was never part of a crowd of deather kids, as they were called where I grew up, around Chapel Hill, NC. There weren't that many, and the ones that were there mostly wouldn't have me. I don't know why. Just wasn't cool enough, I guess. I could never get terribly broken up about it, as I have always enjoyed having a diverse group of friends, not just ones who looked like me, acted like me, and listened to the same music. I think the newer, younger gothic crowd is diversifying a bit, assimilating more types of culture, not just the heavy early-eighties British doomed-out mindset (God love it). I've spent a lot of time at the Cat's Cradle in Chapel Hill, the Fallout Shelter in Raleigh, the 40 Watt Club in Athens, the Blue Crystal and the sadly defunct Robert's La Boucherie in New Orleans.

The New Orleans goth crowd was much nicer to me than the one in Chapel Hill, where I was living at the time I wrote *Lost Souls*. Consequently, the cool deathers in the book are more heavily influenced by them, whereas Nothing's pathetic crowd of school friends in Maryland was largely based on the Chapel Hill scene circa 1987.

What kind of writing implement do you use?

I do most of my work these days on a PC, having been seduced by speed and ease of revision at first, and only later coming to appreciate computers for the fascinating and exotic creatures they are (though I still can't do anything on them but word-process). But I always keep a number of notebooks in which I write and draw by hand, generally in purple ballpoint.

In *Lost Souls,* there are a number of sexual situations both homosexual and heterosexual. Obviously you are comfortable with these subjects so I'd like to ask you about them. Do you feel that, like animals, humans are naturally bisexual? Do you feel that any type of sexual behavior, outside of rape, is unnatural? Do you think S&M between consenting adults is unnatural? In *Lost Souls* there are young children engaging in sexual acts. How do you feel more conservative readers will respond to this? Have you received any negative feedback regarding the sexual situations in *Lost Souls*? In the book you mention Bowie, P. Murphy, et al, who are real bands. Are Lost Souls? a real band as well?

I think humans are naturally *experimental*, anyway. We're all curious. Some of us try things and don't like them all that much, but we'd never know if we hadn't tried, would we? I think some people are naturally gay, some are naturally bi, and some are naturally straight. Nothing is *unnatural*; I find that word meaningless where sex is concerned. We *are* nature. That doesn't mean all nature is good; in fact I think most nature is repellent; I'm a city girl. But I don't have a problem with anything that goes on between consenting people of compatible ages.

I haven't received much negative feedback toward the sexual situations except for being called "amoral," which I choose to take as a compliment. One reviewer pointed out that I was limiting my audience by my affinity for male homosexuals. And that's probably true. But I would limit my audience in some way no matter who I wrote about, unless I chose only bland, featureless characters with no lives whatsoever. I write about the people I love.

And I don't especially *want* homophobes for my audience any more than I would want racists. I mean, if they want to read the book, great; they don't *have* to, and if they do and find something that makes their nuts or ovaries crawl, I offer no apology for that. It's good for them.

I still love the idea of making people consider something in a different light than they would have if they hadn't read my work. If I can make one person question his or her problem with the fact that my characters suck each other's dicks, for Chrissake, that's worth losing any number of pussies who just can't deal with it. I don't want to ram anything down anyone's throat (at least not in writing). Reading is for enjoyment, not propaganda, and if they simply can't enjoy it then they shouldn't read it. But I'm not going to censor myself in deference to anyone else's tastes.

Lost Souls? are only a real band in the alternate universe where Missing Mile, North Carolina appears on the road map. But luckily I get to visit that universe often.

At what age do you think humans should become sexually active?

Preferably before birth, as foetuses in the womb. Hell, foetuses have so many rights these days, why not give 'em the right to conjugal love?

Do you have any physical ideal as far as a partner? (i.e. would your ideal mate or bed partner look like one of the vampires in *Lost Souls*?)

Well . . . I admit I love pale, skinny, hollow-eyed, smooth-skinned, sharp-hipboned, high-cheekboned boys! But no, the vampires in *Lost Souls* started to seem kind of asexual after a while, as if I had spent too much time around them and they had become more like annoying kid brothers or something. I probably wouldn't kick Nothing out of bed. But Steve

Finn is my secret true love. And even more so, one of the main characters of my upcoming novel *Drawing Blood,* a 19-year-old computer hacker fitting the above description. But he already has a boyfriend who I also love dearly.

How did you feel when you found out Abyss was going to publish *Lost Souls*?

I knew someone would publish it. I can't explain how—I'd attempted novels before, which either sucked or didn't get finished, but when I started writing *Lost Souls* I knew this was it. If I was ever going to publish a novel, this would be the one. And I knew I had to start publishing novels, because I couldn't live on short stories and I wasn't fit for any other career. I had no backup plan. But by the day *Lost Souls* went to auction in mid-'91, it had spent so much time sitting on people's desks and all that I just thought it was about time somebody finally wrote me a big old check for the damn thing.

Is there anything else you want to say to the people who will be reading this article?

If you're a member of an incredibly cool, beautiful, insane clique, and you're at the coffeehouse or the club or wherever and see some lonely kid staring with great admiration and longing at your group, please don't cop the patented Black-Eyeliner-Glare-Through-Cigarette-Smoke-"Eat Shit, Geek!" look with matching attitude. If you don't have a friendly word to say or can't risk cracking your deathmask with a smile, just give 'em a sly, knowing nod or something. Who knows? That kid might write your favorite book someday.